D1711908

The Afternoon Snack
La Merienda

Story by
Cuento por

María Luisa Retana

Illustrated by
Ilustrado por

Timothy Adam Valenzuela

High Desert Productions

María L. Retana acknowledges with thanks the support received by her husband Guillermo, and her children Ismael, Talía Alina and Ludim while keeping busy on the project. To her mother, Bertha Valdivia for providing pictures of the author's hometown Colonial Bridge, Puente Yayabo. The pictures were used to create the cover. To Joyce Griffith, owner of Griffith Publishing, for providing advice on how to finance the book. To her far away French friend, Thierry Muller for his input on the essence of the story and for the final revision of the Spanish text. To all of her childhood friends and her sister Iris who inspired her to write the story.

Also the illustrator for this book, Timothy Adam Valenzuela, gives special thanks to, his parents, Joe and Diana Valenzuela for their artistic support, to Marc Valenzuela and Leah Flanningan for modeling for the story's characters, and to Ana María Flanningan for helping on the research about Cuba. To his Tata and Nana, as two beautiful characters in the story. To his family, friends, and roommates for their patience and support. But most important of all, to his Lord Jesus, he thanks for teaching and guiding him throughout this adventure.

The author and illustrator deeply appreciate the financial support given by the New York State Association for Bilingual Education (NYSABE) when publishing this book. Thanks David Mauricio, secretary of the already mentioned organization, for your commitment to this project and your patience when e-mailing back and forth. Diana Valenzuela, we both thank you for editing the manuscript and for being there for us. Special thanks to The Bisbee Arts Commission for granting the illustrator a Professional Development Grant under the category Visual Arts. The grant was used for purchase of art materials. To Dana Dorner, Bisbee High School Art Teacher, for her tremendous involvement and support throughout the entire development of the project. To Joel Anderson owner of Joel Anderson Interesting World Coins (www.joelscoins.com) for the finding of the two Cuban coins: 5 and 10 cents used in the illustrations. To Marty Clemson for letting the author dedicate this book about childhood, laughter and the sharing of snacks to her son Chase. Chase, you will never be forgotten.

ISBN 0-9652920-6-1

Printed in Thailand

In memory of Chase T. Clemson,
the boy who made everyone laugh

En memoria de Chase T. Clemson,
el niño que hizo reír a todos
M.L.R.

To my loving Lord Jesus Christ,
I dedicate the first of all I produce.

Dedico a mi amoroso Señor Jesucristo,
las primicias de mi obra
T.A.V.

The lively peal of a bell is heard. Everyone is on their feet trying to guess who is coming and from which side of San Luis. San Luis is the crossing street from La Onza where, every afternoon, we wait for our snacks to arrive. Who could it be? Is it the ice cream man or the lollipop vendor?

El alegre replico de una campana es oído. Todos están de pie tratando de adivinar quién es el que viene y por cual lado de San Luis. San Luis es la calle que cruza por La Onza donde, cada tarde, esperamos que nos llegue la merienda. ¿Quién será? ¿El heladero o el pirulero?

Manuel runs to the corner of the street and cries out, "They are coming."

Manuel corre a la esquina de la calle y grita, "ahí vienen".

The other children rush home bringing out 10 cents
or two empty glass bottles.

Los demás niños se apresuran a sus casas trayendo
10 centavos o dos botellas de vidrio vacías.

The vendors are now almost around the corner. First, the ice cream man and his ice cream cart appear.

Los vendedores ya están casi en la esquina. Primero, aparece el heladero con su carrito de helado.

Los que han escogido tener helado lo rodean. El resto de la pandilla ha corrido un poquito mas cuesta abajo por San Luis para alcanzar al pirulero y su carretilla.

The ones who choose ice cream surround him. The rest of the gang has run a little further down San Luis to meet the lollipop vendor and his handcart.

The gang wants to know what ice cream flavors he has brought today. The ice cream man makes sure that they have their 10 cents with them.

La pandilla quiere saber que sabores de helado a traído hoy. El heladero se asegura que ellos tienen los 10 centavos consigo.

Manuel, Abel y yo hemos alcanzado al pirulero y su carretilla así que gritamos: "Oye pirulero, ¿qué clase de pirulíes tienes hoy?" Grita a voz en cuello, "melón, naranja, limón, café." ¡Qué genio! Tiene la cara como un tomate y se oye ronco.

Manuel, Abel and I have reached the lollipop vendor and his handcart and so we yell: "Hey lollipop vendor, what kind of lollipops do you have today?" He shouts out over our voices, "watermelon, orange, lemon, coffee." What a temper! His face is red as a tomato and his voice is hoarse.

He wants us to get in line with our money in our hands or two empty glass bottles. Only then can we choose our lollipops.

Quiere que nos pongamos en fila con el dinero en la mano o dos botellas de vidrio vacías. Solo entonces podremos escoger nuestros pirulíes.

Los vendedores siguen su camino y nosotros corremos al portal de Manuel.

The vendors move on and we run to Manuel's porch.

We sit at the edge of the porch showing off the ice cream or lollipop flavors we got.

Nos sentamos a la orilla del portal mostrando los sabores de helado y pirulí que obtuvimos.

Aleida y Kiko están comiendo helado de vainilla en un barquillo. La paleta que se le está derritiendo a Norberto es de melón. La de Iris es de naranja pero se las arregla para morder la paleta de sabor a chocolate que Barbarita ya lleva por la mitad.

Aleida and Kiko are eating vanilla ice cream in a cone. Norberto's melting popsicle is watermelon flavor. Iris' popsicle is orange flavor but she managed to get a bite of Barbarita's half eaten chocolate one.

Our hands are getting sticky. The gang is simply sharing their snacks as not to miss any of the ice cream and the lollipop vendor's flavors of the day.

Las manos se nos están poniendo pegajosas. La pandilla está compartiendo su merienda para así no perderse ninguno de los sabores del día que trajeron el heladero y el pirulero.

De pronto, el cielo se pone negro y grandes gotas de agua acompañadas de relámpagos y truenos, hacen que corramos a nuestras casas.

Suddenly, the sky turns black and big raindrops, accompanied by lighting and thunder, make us run to our homes.

Iris and I, from the living room's slatted shutters, can see Manuel, Kiko, Aleida and Barbarita in front of their porch under the rain, laughing.

Iris y yo, desde los postigos de la ventana que está en la sala, podemos ver a Manuel, Kiko, Aleida y Barbarita en frente del portal bajo el aguacero, riéndose.

Mañana voy a comerme un barquillo de helado de chocolate.

Tomorrow I'll have a chocolate ice cream cone.

About the Author/ Sobre la Autora

María Luisa Retana was born in Cuba. She received her B.A. in Spanish and Comparative Literature from the University of California, Riverside. She has worked extensively with children of all ages in scholastic and cultural events as well as in theater. Mrs. Retana lives with her husband and three children in Bisbee, Arizona. She is also the author of 3 published bilingual children's books and the owner and publisher of High Desert Productions, a small independent press located in Bisbee, Az.

María Luisa Retana nació en Cuba. Se recibió con una licenciatura en Literatura Española y Comparada de la Universidad de California en Riverside. Ha trabajado extensamente con niños de todas las edades en eventos escolares, y culturales e igualmente en teatro. La Sra. Retana vive con su esposo y tres hijos en Bisbee, Arizona. También es la autora de 3 libros bilingües para niños y la propietaria y Editora de High Desert Productions, una imprenta modesta e independiente situada en Bisbee, Az.

About the Illustrator/Sobre el Ilustrador

Timothy Adam Valenzuela is the son of Joe Pete and Diana Valenzuela, and was born in Bisbee, Arizona. He is eighteen years old and graduated from Bisbee High School in the year 2000. "The Afternoon Snack" is Timothy's first professional project. At seventeen years old he began illustrating for the project. Timothy currently lives in Phoenix, Arizona attending Southwestern Bible College of Phoenix and has future plans to major in Computer Animation.

Timothy Adam Valenzuela es hijo de Joe Pete y Diana Valenzuela, y nació en Bisbee, Arizona. Tiene dieciocho años, y se graduó de Bisbee High School en el año 2000. "La merienda" es el primer proyecto profesional de Timothy, y a los diecisiete años empezó a ilustrar para éste. En la actualidad Timothy vive en Phoenix, Arizona donde asiste al colegio "Southwestern Bible College of Phoenix," y piensa especializarse en Animación por Computación.

NEW YORK STATE ASSOCIATION FOR BILINGUAL EDUCATION

**Eugenio Maria de Hostos Community College
of the City University of New York
Division of Academic Affairs
500 Grand Concourse, B-447
Bronx, New York 10451**

www.nysabe.org

The purpose of NYSABE is to encourage the establishment, maintenance, and expansion of quality programs of bilingual education through which students will be provided with the opportunity to develop bilingualism; to promote bilingual education as a logical education process and approach by which success on the part of all students is enhanced through learning in their first language while they are learning to function in their second language; to promote recognition by the total community of the importance of bilingualism and its contributions toward better understanding among people; and to promote bilingual instruction, with recognition that the teaching of language skills and the enhancement of conceptual growth is most meaningful and effective when presented with an awareness and appreciation of the strengths of cultural and linguistic differences among people.

I, Timothy Adam Valenzuela, illustrator for The Afternoon Snack/La merienda, would like to share my experience with the reader when illustrating this book. Through out my life I always found ways to express my feelings using my creative side. My general intention for "La merienda" was to illustrate for the readers an experience in Cuba within the natural life of a young child.

My choice of mediums for this project was truly unique. At the beginning of the project I dreamed of doing something truly special for the illustrations. I imagined a group of laughing children completely amazed while turning the pages of the book. I thought of the needs of children today, and wanted to reach them at their level. It was also my desire for the audience to experience something they have never experienced before. With these thoughts in mind I took the first of my hand drawn pictures and scanned them to the computer. After weeks of experimenting with new approaches using computer art programs, I found that enhancing my hand drawn pictures on the computer was what I was looking for.

The method of computer art that I chose for this project was a very challenging task to execute. The most common method of drawing is everything within an illustration is drawn on the same page as one whole drawing. In my case, I drew each tiny detail of every illustration piece by piece on separate sheets of paper. Every character, door, window, palm tree, pillar, and little rock in my illustrations were drawn separately. The reason for this was that on the computer I had the freedom to position shadows properly and change any detail producing a more perfect final product.

The wonderful opportunity to illustrate a bilingual book has taught me many things about life. I have a joyous feeling in my heart to be a part of producing a book, that children of different cultures can share together. It is a joy to know that children that are struggling with two languages, or seeking to learn a second language will benefit from something that I created. I have learned that hard work and dedication, at the end, does pay off. No matter how challenging a project might seem, one must stick with whatever the process might be and never give up. By remaining completely focused with faith in God, anything can be accomplished.

Please Email me with any questions or comments at: timothyadam2000@yahoo.com
Phone at: 1-520-432-2719
Or write to: Timothy Adam Valenzuela, 226 Park Avenue, Bisbee Arizona 85603

High Desert Productions is a small independent press located in Bisbee, Arizona. We specialize in Multicultural/Bilingual children's books.

Now in Print

The Pig That is Not a Pig/El cerdo que no es cerdo

Written by María Luisa Retana
Illustrated by Marian Weaver

Born Into The Pack/Nacer en la manada

Written by María Luisa Retana
Translated by Guillermo Retana
Illustrated by Marian Weaver

Tall Tails From a Mountain Slope/Los rabos altos de la ladera

Written by María Luisa Retana
Translated by Guillermo Retana
Illustrated by Marian Weaver

Coming Soon From High Desert Productions

Tanilí
(An afro-cuban folktale during post-slavery times)

Retold by María Luisa Retana & Mary Ann Hanson-Germond
Illustrated by Mary Ann Hanson-Germond

To place an order feel free to:

Email us at: hdproductions50@hotmail.com
View us at: http://hdp50.users1.50megs.com/welcome.html